Harriet Ziefert & Seymour Chwast

Ode To Humpty Dumpty

OUR HERO

HOUGHTON MIFFLIN COMPANY BOSTON 2001

Walter Lorraine Books

For James and Jennifer   H. Z.
For little Kyle   S. C.

Walter Lorraine (wx) Books

Text copyright © 2001 by Harriet Ziefert
Illustrations copyright © 2001 by Seymour Chwast

Library of Congress Cataloging-in-Publication Data

Ziefert, Harriet.
    Ode to Humpty Dumpty / by Harriet Ziefert: Illustrated by Seymour Chwast.
    p. cm.
    Summary: After failing to save Humpty Dumpty, the King's friends find
different ways to help him deal with his grief.
    ISBN 0-618-05047-7
    [1. Characters in literature – Fiction.] I. Chwast, Seymour, ill. II. Title.
PZ8.3.Z47 Od 2001
[E]—dc21   99-048647

Printed in China for Harriet Ziefert, Inc.
HZI 10 9 8 7 6 5 4 3 2 1

Humpty Dumpty sat on a wall;
Humpty Dumpty had a great fall.

All the King's horses and all the King's men,
Couldn't put Humpty together again.

Doctor, Doctor, hurry quick!
Humpty Dumpty's very sick.

"It's sad to say, but I know quite well,
Bandages won't mend poor Humpty's shell."

The baker brushed with a flour paste,
But he knew his efforts were a waste.

"Humpty's shell is badly broke,
And he's losing all his yolk!"

With needle and thread the tailor arrived.
But he knew that Humpty had not survived.

He put on his glasses and began to shout,
"Humpty Dumpty's insides will soon be out!"

The King knew Humpty
would never get better.
He cried till his eyes got
redder and redder.

Norma Jean Foote,
creative and smart,
Knew how to mend
a King's broken heart.

She asked a builder from down the street:
"Can you build an egg house all tidy and neat?"

"I'll build an egg house all tidy and neat,
A perfect place for the King's friends to meet!"

She found the sculptor, Harold von Bleek.
Her eyes filled with tears as she started to speak.

"Make us a statue from perfect white stone
Of a happy Humpty near a King's throne."

Then she said to the gardener, Reginald Leaf,
"We need something growing to soften our grief."

Said the gardener, "Ms. Foote, I want you to see,
I've shaped a beautiful H. Dumpty tree."

The gardener's assistant
knew what to make,
A Humpty slide by the
side of the lake.

"We'll have a playground,
all tidy and neat,
Where the King's children
can frolic and meet."

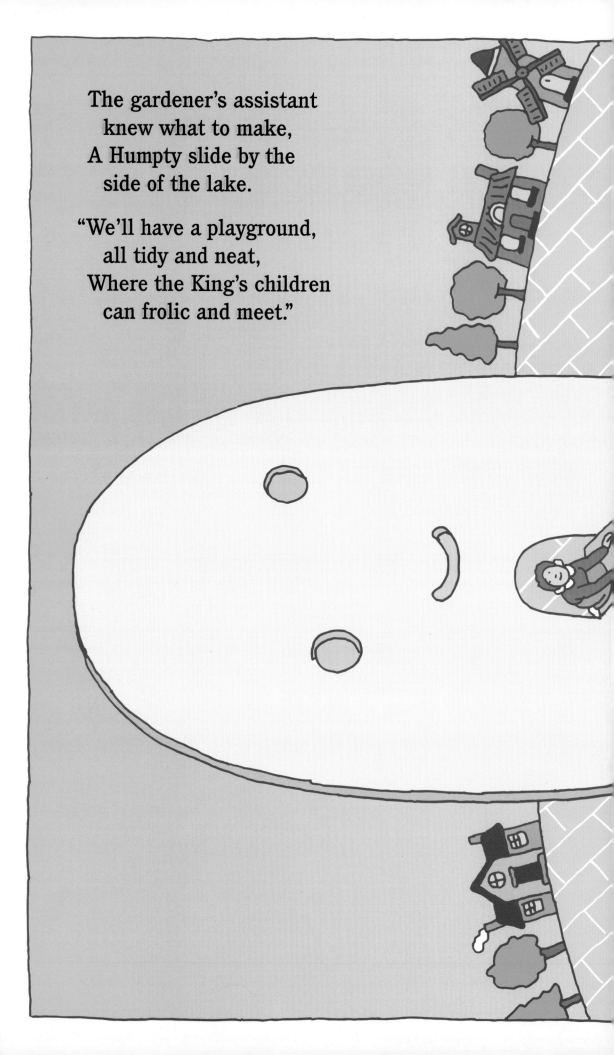

A committee planned a Dumpty Museum;
The cooks concocted Humpty ice cream.

The seamstresses stitched Humpty-shaped pillows;
The gardener planted more H. Dumpty willows.

The town crier called, "Come one and come all!
There's going to be a Great Humpty Ball.

You're invited to dance, to eat, and to sing.
We'll all honor Humpty and cheer up the King."

The statue was finished;
   the house was all done.
The gardens looked perfect
   in the bright sun.

          Everyone fell silent;
             they formed a huge ring.
          They sang *Ode to Humpty*,
             led by the King.

Humpty Dumpty sat on a wall;
We thought that Humpty would never fall.
Happy we were, as we passed by,
To see Humpty Dumpty framed by the sky.

Humpty Dumpty had a kind face;
He always behaved with honor and grace.
We said Humpty was our national treasure,
Who looked down on us with unending pleasure.

Humpty Dumpty sat on a wall;
Humpty Dumpty had a great fall.
We cried and cried and were heard to mutter,
"Our wonderful Humpty lies in the gutter."

Humpty Dumpty had a great fall.
He couldn't be saved, though we tried, one and all.

Now we have Humpty in house, song, and tree,

Humpty now lives in loving memory.